Good Day, Good Night

To Griffith and Graham, the two little boys I read *Goodnight Moon* to
over and over and over.
—L.L.

First published in hardback in the USA by HarperCollins Children's Books,
a division of HarperCollins Publishers, New York, in 2017.
First published in hardback in Great Britain by HarperCollins Children's Books,
a division of HarperCollins Publishers Ltd., in 2017.
This paperback edition first published in Great Britain in 2018.

1 3 5 7 9 10 8 6 4 2

ISBN: 978-0-00-826121-4

Text copyright © Hollins University 2017
Illustrations copyright © Loren Long 2017

The artist used acrylics on illustration board to create the illustrations for this book.
Typography by Jean L. Hogle

Visit our website at: www.harpercollins.co.uk
Printed and bound in China

Good Day, Good Night

By MARGARET WISE BROWN

Pictures by LOREN LONG

HarperCollins *Children's Books*

When the sun came up the day began.
Who saw the first light of the sun?
"I," said a bunny, "the only one."

Good morning, world!

Hello, daylight

Good day, everyone

Goodbye, night

Good day, trees
And birds in the skies

Good day, bees
Buzz out of your hives

Good day, kitty
There's milk in your cup

Stretch, little cat
Try to wake up

Good morning to you!
Open your eyes
For every day
Is a new surprise

Go live your day!

When the moon came up the night began.

Good night, birds
Down in your nest

Good night, bees
Time to rest

Good night, sky
And the daylight
Good night, flowers
Bugs, good night

Good night, kitty
Good night, bear

Good night, people
everywhere

Good night, toys
Good night, world
Under the covers
I cuddle and curl

The rabbit twitched his nose
And his ruby eyes closed
Good night, little bunny
Go to sleep.